The BookMann Family in...

Book 1

Don't Judge a Book by its Cover
by Lisa Edman Lamote

BookMann press — An imprint of the mann

PUBLISHED BY
BookMann Press - An imprint of the Mann Publishing Group
710 Main Street, 6th Floor
PO Box 580
Rollinsford, NH 03869 USA
www.mannpublishing.com
www.askopus.com
+1 (603) 601-0325

ISBN: 1-933673-01-X
Library of Congress Control Number (LCCN): 2006923129
Printed and bound in Hong Kong.
10 9 8 7 6 5 4 3 2 1

CREDITS

Author:	Lisa Edman Lamote
Illustrations:	MyIllustration.com, Alisha Wilson
Series Concept:	Anthony T. Mann
Cover Design:	Marcelo Paiva
Special Thanks:	Jeff Edman, Alison Mann, Bernard Lamote,
	Molly Barnaby, & Bob Greiza

meet The BookMann Family

The BookMann Family lives in a library, where they experience adventures as they interact with the outside world and the people who borrow them. Each member of the family is a specific type of book.

BookMann is a book about computers. He is the father of the family. BookMann is borrowed frequently and is very popular. He is smart, fair, honest, and thinks very logically.

Thesis is a book about history. She is the mother of the family. She is also the wife of BookMann and the daughter of Opus. She loves to teach and learn new subjects.

Opus is the reference encyclopedia for the library. He is Thesis' father, and the grandfather of the family. He is old and wise and knows practically everything. He cannot be borrowed from the library. He strolls about his library home, using a ruler for a walking stick.

Pamphlet is a book about fashion design. She is talkative and clever, but can sometimes be a bit bossy. She is 12 years old, and can often be found talking on her cell phone with her best friend Glossy.

Booklet is a book about the history of baseball. He is very active with his friends. Booklet can also be rather shy and tries to hide his bashfulness with a tough and scrappy attitude. He is 7 years old.

Tablet is an electronic book recently adopted into the BookMann Family. He can do wonderful things on his writable computer screen, and can plug into the Internet. He is 4 years old and wants to be just like his big brother Booklet.

Leaflet is a document for reference only, which means that he is never borrowed from the library. As an infant, he is naturally curious about his library world. He wears a diaper, clipped with a paper clip instead of a safety pin.

It is a beautiful day in the park outside the library. The sun is shining and birds are fluttering overhead and singing in the trees. The smell of cut grass is in the air. Summer has arrived. It is a perfect day to enjoy a game of baseball. And that's just what Booklet and his friends are doing.

Booklet's sister Pamphlet arrives in the park and sees the boys at play on the baseball field. They are laughing as they round the diamond and hustle in the outfield. Pamphlet sees a group of her friends sitting under a tree nearby and waves, but doesn't go over to them. "Today," Pamphlet thinks, "I feel like doing something different. Today, I feel like playing baseball."

In fact, Pamphlet has been thinking for a long
time that she'd like to try playing baseball.
"I might even like to join a team," she thinks. "After
all, it looks like such fun and it's very good exercise."
Today seems like a perfect day for it, so she approaches
the boys on the field and asks, "Hey guys, may I play too?"

"You?" replies Pulp, a young book with a nasty expression, as if something stinky has just crawled under his nose. "But you're a girl! Girls can't play baseball!"

"Yeah," objects another book, "and you're not even a book about sports!"

"Why don't you go and play with your dolls?" spits Pulp. Booklet shifts his feet uncomfortably, looking from his sister Pamphlet to his friend Pulp.

Pamphlet walks away slowly, feeling rejected. Booklet watches her go, as the other boys return to their game, but says nothing. This is not the response that Pamphlet expected. Boy or girl, sports book or other book, what difference does it make? What disappointed her most, though, was that they didn't even give her a chance.

Pamphlet joins her friends under a nearby tree.
They have just witnessed the scene on the baseball field. She tells
them exactly what happened.
"That book Pulp is just rotten!" says Pamphlet's best friend, Glossy,
who is also a fashion book. "Ooh, I feel like going over there and
rearranging his index!"

"No, Glossy," warns Pamphlet. "Violence is never the answer."

"In his case, I'd be willing to make an exception," says Glossy sourly.

"And you know," adds Pamphlet, "now that they told me I can't play, I want to play even more! Why is that?"

"Well what are you going to do?" asks Glossy.

"I don't know," answers Pamphlet.

"Usually, when I don't know what to do—Hey, that's it! I'll ask Opus!"

Back in the library, Booklet is troubled. He goes to his mom, Thesis, and tells her what happened on the baseball field. "I guess Pulp was kind of hard on her," he admits. "And what did you say?" Thesis asks.

"Well, I…" Booklet hangs his head until his chin is almost touching his cover. "Nothing," he answers. Thesis looks at him and says gently, "I see."

"But Mom, girls aren't even supposed to like baseball!" he objects. "And why not?" Thesis responds. "You both like reading, and flying kites, and riding bikes. Why can't you both like baseball?"

"Well…I…I don't know…" Booklet stutters, "because she's…she's a…" But somehow, he can't finish.
"Listen Booklet. I know how much it hurts to be left out without being given a chance," confides Thesis softly.

"A while ago, I invited my friend Raja Recipe—you know her, the nice Indian cookbook—to join our weekly book club. But the other members rejected her because, well…they said she was…only a cookbook."

"Gosh," breathes Booklet softly, shocked. "Yes, well, it was very hurtful to Raja, and I was very disappointed in my friends," says Thesis.

"What did you do?" asks Booklet.

"Well, Raja was too shy to stand up for herself, so, as her friend, I did it for her," says Thesis. "I told them if they weren't the kind of books that would give Raja a chance, then I refused to be in a club like that."

"You did?"

"Yes, I did. And it worked! They gave her a chance to speak and they all loved her! She'll be our vice-president next month!"

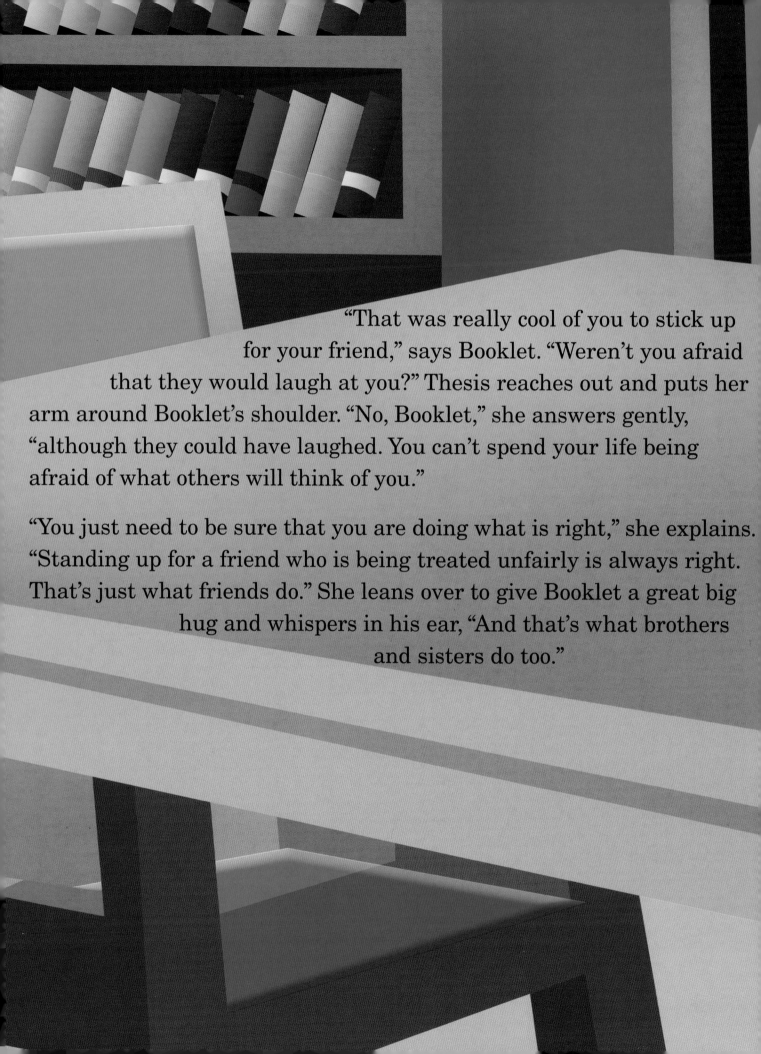

"That was really cool of you to stick up for your friend," says Booklet. "Weren't you afraid that they would laugh at you?" Thesis reaches out and puts her arm around Booklet's shoulder. "No, Booklet," she answers gently, "although they could have laughed. You can't spend your life being afraid of what others will think of you."

"You just need to be sure that you are doing what is right," she explains. "Standing up for a friend who is being treated unfairly is always right. That's just what friends do." She leans over to give Booklet a great big hug and whispers in his ear, "And that's what brothers and sisters do too."

Meanwhile, Pamphlet learns that Opus is helping in the reading corner of the library today. As she arrives, she sees many young books listening intently as Opus concludes, "…and that is why there's a rainbow after it rains." The young books clap for Opus and then get up to leave.

Opus turns and sees Pamphlet. "Why, hello Pamphlet," he greets her. Then, noticing her expression, he asks, "Hey, why the long cover? Is there a problem?"

"Yes, Grandpa Opus, there is," she answers. "May I talk to you?"

"I always have time for you, Pamphlet, dear," says Opus lovingly. "Just ask Opus and we'll find an answer together."

A Day Out for Opus

CLIPS CLIPS IPS

Pamphlet recounts the events on the baseball field. She is upset that her own brother didn't stand up for her. "I guess he didn't want to look stupid in front of his friends, but still…" she says. "Ah, yes," agrees Opus, "people sometimes do silly things to impress their friends. Unfortunately, there will always be books who will take one look at us and decide very quickly, and usually quite incorrectly, what we can and cannot do. There's always some book ready to reject someone who's a little different."

"But why would someone do that?" asks Pamphlet.
"I guess they think it's easier than getting to know someone and giving them a chance. They don't realize that keeping your mind open can also open up lots of fun possibilities," explains Opus patiently.
"I understand how hurtful it can be when someone doesn't believe in you," he continues. "Unfortunately, it happens to all of us sometimes."
"I bet it doesn't happen to you, Grandpa Opus. Everyone knows you know everything. Besides, grown-ups would never behave that way!" exclaims Pamphlet. "Oh, wouldn't they?" says Opus questioningly.

"Last year, when I wanted to be on the team of judges that chooses the library's Recommended Reading List, they took one look at me and said I was too old to know what young readers want these days," tells Opus. "But I knew that my years of experience would be useful to the group. After all, I know more about what goes on in this library than anyone."

"But Grandpa Opus," interrupts Pamphlet, "you *are* one of the judges. How did you convince them?"

"I wouldn't give up, that's how!" reveals Opus. "I wasn't about to lie down on the shelf and accept that kind of treatment. I did the only thing a book could do. I stood up for myself! I brushed off my dust cover, marched back in and told them my ideas. I also said that sometimes old books are just as valuable as new books. They were so impressed, they let me on the team then and there."

"You see, Pamphlet," begins Opus, "if you let others tell you that you can't do something, soon you'll start to believe them. And by letting them turn you away with their quick judgements, you're not doing them any favors either, because they'll never learn to open their hearts to those who are different."

"You're right, Grandpa Opus," Pamphlet realizes.

"Standing up for
yourself is better for
everyone. I feel so much
better just by talking it over with
you. You really do know everything!"
"Well, not quite, but I try, dear," concedes
Opus.
Pamphlet decides, "I'm going to go back to the ball
field and make them give me a chance!"
"That's my girl!" beams Opus.

Pamphlet returns to the field, jumps up on a tree stump and says, "I think it's unfair of you not to even give me a chance. And I'm not leaving until you let me try!"

"We told you before, this game's not for you," insists Pulp. But this time, Booklet steps up, joins Pamphlet at the tree stump and says, "She's right guys. Everyone deserves a chance."

"Why should we?" asks Pulp.

"Because it's the right thing to do," answers Booklet. "If this game isn't open to everyone, then I don't want to play anymore. Come on Pamphlet, let's go." The two of them begin to leave.

"OK, don't get your pages all bent out of shape about it," says Pulp. "She can play, but she's on your team!"

"Deal!" say Booklet and Pamphlet together.

It's another beautiful day in the park and all the books have turned up to watch a baseball game. The BookMann family sits in the stands watching excitedly. Everyone is enjoying the game, especially the kids. Booklet and Pamphlet have both played a great game and Pamphlet comes up to her last time at bat. "Come on, Pamphlet!" yells BookMann, waving encouragingly.

"That's my girl!" calls Opus proudly. The score is tied and everyone waits to see how the game will end. Pamphlet steps up to the plate. She knows her team is counting on her. She hears Booklet and her other team mates cheering her on and…CRACK! She hits the ball and it goes soaring, higher and higher, right out of the park!

The crowd is cheering wildly. Books of
every variety rush out onto the field as
Pamphlet's teammates lift her up onto
their shoulders and sweep her away for
a victory lap around the diamond.

Through the crowd, Pulp approaches Pamphlet, who is still on the boys' shoulders. He looks up at her to exclaim, "Well, flip my pages! You're really good! You can be on my team any time!"

"Thanks Pulp, I appreciate that," replies Pamphlet, looking over at Booklet, "but I think I'll stick with the team that believed in me from the start."

After things have calmed down, the BookMann family is reunited on the field. "We are so proud of you both," says BookMann.

"Yeah, it was a great game," replies Booklet.

"No, not for the game," says Thesis, "For what you've both learned here. To stand up to intolerance and do the right thing, even when—especially when—it means risking ridicule or embarrassment."

Pamphlet turns to Booklet with a bright smile on her face. "Thanks for standing up for me, Booklet…and for believing in me." "I'm just sorry I didn't do it sooner," he replies. Opus looks at the two of them fondly and says, "It just goes to show that you can miss out on a lot of great things when you make the mistake of judging a book by its cover."

The BookMann Family

For more adventures, check out these books...

Book 2:
Booklet Goes to the Doctor

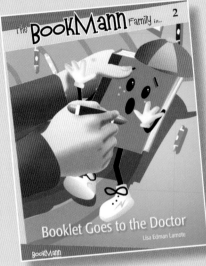

Young Booklet is checked out of the library and damaged by a young child who marks him up with a crayon. So begins Booklet's trip to see Dr. Binder, the book doctor. Along the way, Booklet meets new friends who have also had problems with readers who don't know how to treat books with respect. Booklet must deal with his embarrassment about his crayon marks, and overcome his fear of going to the dreaded doctor's office.

Book 3:
A Day Out for Opus

Grandfather Opus is a little down because he never leaves the library. To boost his spirits, the family organizes a "trip around the world" by visiting different sections of the library and learning about all the new experiences that are possible through the pages of books. They climb the Eiffel Tower, tour the Zambezi River in Africa, and see the Pyramids. Opus and the family realize that new adventures are theirs for the taking, right there in the local library.

For more information on the BookMann Family, visit

www.AskOpus.com

BookMann press